TWICE LOVE BURNED

Rhea Ryan

For those that dream, dream big.

AUTHOR'S NOTE

The Bone Love Duet is two books. Think of Twice Love Burned as a 1.5 bonus chapter. Although the events of this instalment happen prior to Pretty Little Island, this story was written to be enjoyed after Pretty Little Island. If you have not yet read Pretty Little Island, please stop now, and go read it as Twice Love Burned contains spoilers. It's currently available on Kindle Unlimited.

If you've already read Pretty Little Island, I promise a fulfilling conclusion to the story is forthcoming. In the meantime, enjoy!

This isn't a regular love story, and it doesn't have a happy ending.

My bond with my twin was impenetrable, until a blonde femme fatale walked into the party, capturing our attention and burying her way into our hearts.

As Olivia took control of our lives, the three of us forged an unconventional relationship that fooled everyone—including ourselves.

But it wasn't meant to last.

One moment, one mistake, one bad decision, and my world shattered to pieces.

Olivia was never meant to be mine, and she never was, even though I was the last person to see her alive.

Trigger Warnings

Non-Consent
    Drug Use
    Underage Sex
    Gore
    Death
    Choking
    Underage Drinking

CHAPTER ONE

1.5 Years Before the Plane Crash

Micah

The party at Ezra's has already started by the time Maison and I walk in. Everyone parts ways to let us through and cheers, patting us on the back from our big win tonight. We are like kings in this school, and my family runs this entire town. Whenever we walk in somewhere, the party really starts, and everyone stares and kisses our asses like they should.

Maison and I settle in the living room with the music blaring around me. Everyone is borderline wasted already. New Ocean is the place to be tonight, and Ezra's dad generously offered us his house, spending the entire weekend in the city, leaving us full access.

What a stupid motherfucker. Every single bed will end up getting fucked in—and I doubt anyone knows how to do laundry.

"Good win tonight, fuckers," Maison says, pouring a shot of Jack Daniels into his mouth before handing me the bottle. Maison likes to celebrate, usually with a drink, or ten. He jabs Ezra's side, who he's seated next to. "Congrats on your first big goal, buddy." He lays a lazy arm around Ezra and shoots me a glance to shut my mouth.

Leave it to Maison to play the middleman, but I'd rather choke on acid than congratulate Ezra on what should have been mine. We won the city championships for the third year in a row. New Ocean Prep never won a single tournament before I joined the team. I should be thrilled about our victory, considering I put this school on the map.

Except I'm fucking not.

Six scouts came to watch me tonight. They weren't there to watch anyone else—just me. And all I did was royally screw it up. I had a chance for a hat trick and to score the winning goal as I usually do. Instead, I got caught up in some bullshit, and my temper got the best of me when a fucker on the Douglas Cove team messed with Maison. They fuck with him to fuck with me, and I let them get to me.

Every. Single. Damn. Time.

Instead of living my moment, I spent the last two minutes in the penalty box because I pulled his helmet off and punched the shit out of him. Ezra ended up scoring the winning goal, and he shouldn't have been on the ice. He's a year younger than me and a first-year on the senior team. He needs to earn his place, not try to take mine. Maison fed him the goal—of course it was Maison, and it was a short-handed goal which makes it sting even worse.

Even though it felt good to punch the other team out, it took every inch of control not to throw down on Ezra, too, and wipe that smug look off his face as he skated by me. He gloated about it for ten minutes in the dressing room after. If Maison wasn't there to babysit him, I would have broken his fucking nose. I don't give a shit if our parents have been friends for years.

Ezra sits across from me and next to Maison with a mocking smirk still planted on his angular face. Maison gives me a knowing look and instead of firing an insult at the kid, I say nothing. I still plan on fucking with Ezra tonight, even if Maison doesn't want me to. His little girlfriend Naomi has pined over me for years, and tonight I plan on shoving my dick in her mouth. I don't give a shit if we are at his house. She shamelessly flirts with me in front of him anyway, which is part of the reason we don't like each other. I used to kick his ass as a kid, which is probably another reason.

When I'm done with her, I'll make sure her panties are wet because it's my dick she's thinking about when she goes home and touches herself. And rumor has it, Ezra hasn't even sealed the deal with her yet. She's a token virgin.

I avoid Ezra's annoying face and chat with Thomas instead. He's a bigger kid—and doesn't say much, which I like. He's the only younger kid on the team with any sort of talent. And he's loyal to me. He never tries to outshine me on the ice like Ezra does. He only backs me up.

A couple of cute girls walk by the couch, giggling and smiling at us. Ezra mutters some dirty words at them while I search for Naomi, who's chatting with her friend Serena across the room, still wearing their cheer outfits, her blonde ponytail swaying around. Ezra's such a fucker. By the way, he's eye fucking all the chicks here. It looks like he and Naomi are off right now. It doesn't take her long to make eye contact with me, and I know Ezra's noticed.

Maison turns to me and grins, lifting each brow. "Time to party, bro," he says as he flashes a smile at them. I ignore them, which is my usual MO. Although I enjoy the skimpy outfits they are wearing. Bras as shirts seem to be the new thing—and I don't hate it. The girls in this town are boring, same old song and dance every weekend. And I really dislike talking. It's much easier to stay quiet.

"Take it easy, Maison," I say, "the night's still young."

Maison's like a kid in a candy store when it comes to chicks. He's always been a bigger slut than me. He falls fast and hard, then moves on like it didn't happen. I don't want or have time for a girlfriend right now. Hockey is my number one and will be till I get scouted.

I can't fuck it up again.

I have to get myself under control and prove to my parents getting myself off those fucking meds was the best thing for me. That I can control the anger and sadness that overwhelms me sometimes without medicating myself to do it. The meds leave my body weak and my mind clouded. I don't fuck the same on them; they take away every ounce of my libido. And if I don't have sex—I can't fucking breathe.

Sex and hockey—the only two things I think about.

My twin leans back on the couch, giving the girls a playful smile as they continue to undress us with their eyes, shifting their gaze between the two of us. It was Maison's idea to dress identically tonight. He knows how irritated people make me, and sometimes it's fun taking a break being me. While our personalities couldn't be more different, we've mastered each other's quirks. There is only one real physical difference. The scar on Maison's shoulder. The cause of my lingering PTSD and the reason I'm so fucked up.

People treat us differently, especially when they have no idea who they are actually speaking to. I can weed out the fake ones easier, so we opted for a white T-shirt and jeans. The white drives the girls crazy because it brings out our natural tan on our olive skin. And the T-shirt—I'm well aware of what we look like. We train hard for these muscles and since we both sprouted two inches last year, Maison and I are the biggest guys on the team.

It doesn't take long for the girls to flock to us. Naomi and her friend Serena walk by and smile at us. Ezra nearly lurches off his seat.

Desperate prick.

Serena seems to have it bad for Maison. She turns red as a cherry every time he smiles at her. I'm about to wave them over, but another blonde catches my attention. One I haven't seen around here before. She walks into the party with a friend who leaves her, and she immediately huddles to the corner and picks up her phone, glancing at it. A sure sign she doesn't know anyone here, which also makes her an easy target. Because she's hot—like seriously fucking hot. Tall, slim, and generously proportioned. She's obviously dying for people to look at her. Her tits are pressed up high in that low-cut shirt, and her ass is meaty in those tight jeans. She dressed to impress.

I recognize her from somewhere; I know I do.

So, who is she?

I'm not the only one who's noticed. Ezra and Maison are already pointing and grinning. Probably scheming on which one of them is going to hit on her first. I'll sit back and watch this one play out. I don't have the energy for drama, and I don't chase girls.

Maison waves her over. Both Ezra and Maison can't rip their eyes from her. I know who my money's on. Maison keeps jerking his chin till she narrows her eyes as if realizing it's her he's calling. She walks toward us and stands in front of the couch, cutting her gaze over to me, then back to them, parting her lips slightly.

Yeah, sweetheart—there are two of us.

Maison smiles at her while I stare, trying to figure out where I know her from.

"What's your name, sexy?" Ezra cuts in like a scumbag.

She darts her eyes to him, then back to Maison. "Olivia."

Sexy voice, Olivia.

Maison leans back. "Olivia. Pretty name."

She twirls a lock of her hair and smiles. And he's got her—hook, line, and sinker. He nudges Ezra over. "Sit down, Olivia. Don't stand by yourself in the dark corner. You're too pretty to stand there alone. I'll protect you from all the fuckers at this party who are staring at you." He elbows Ezra.

"What the fuck, man," Ezra grits out at and moves away from Maison. "This is my fucking house. I'll stare at who I want."

That's part of Ezra's problem—he's too fucking eager.

Maison is as well, but girls flock to him, anyway. It's like he puts out some sort of pheromone like a dog in heat. He gives them a playful smile, and they feel all safe with him. A short time later, their tongues are usually down his throat.

That's something I don't do. I haven't smiled a day in my life. Girls seem to like me for a completely different reason.

She lifts her eyebrows and darts her gaze to me again, adjusting her purse on her shoulder. "I don't know if that's a good idea," she says. "I'm not supposed to be here; my friends would be furious. You're part of the rival team."

That's it.

She's the girlfriend of the fucker I punched out at today's game. The hot blonde I always see in the stands when we play Douglas Cove.

Number eleven—their team captain—last name, Fitzgerald.

I don't remember seeing her at the game tonight. So, why is she here at a New Ocean celebration party? I can't help myself. "So, where's your boyfriend, Olivia?" I lounge back with my hands around my head lazily. I keep my voice neutral.

She whips her head toward me, and her green eyes flash. "I don't have a boyfriend. We broke up. I'm here because my friend was invited, and I didn't want her to come here alone."

Since her friend is not around, I can only assume she's upstairs somewhere—invited by someone.

I cock my brow. "So nice of you." She's here for a reason. Girls from Douglas Cove don't just show up to our parties.

Maison shoots me a back the fuck off look. "Don't listen to him," he says. "I want you here."

Maison's always the nice guy.

He leans forward and grabs her a beer from a stockpile he has at his feet. "Sit down, baby, have a drink with me and celebrate with the winning team."

She smiles and sits down next to him, her tension immediately easing. She crosses her legs and runs her hands down her long, wavy, blonde hair, tucking it behind her heart-shaped face.

Fuck, she's gorgeous.

Maison does his lip biting thing and puts his arm around her as she sits and leans a bit into him. "Were you at the game tonight?" he asks.

She smiles and nods. "I was actually. My friend and I drove in for it."

She must have been hiding. I don't remember her there. She's always wearing number eleven and is in the front row. Maybe she and Fitzgerald really broke up.

"Did you see my goal?" he asks, rubbing his hand on her thigh.

She gives him a slow smile and nods, completely ignoring me, even though I scored two fucking goals tonight.

It's over—guarantee he'll fuck her within an hour.

She continues her hair-twirling flirty gestures, and Ezra fucks off toward where Naomi is hanging out. Maison gives me a beat it face, so I get up and give him his space. He'll be consumed with this chick all night now.

The next hour is a flurry of shots, beer, and basic debauchery as New Ocean's finest destroy Ezra's dad's house. I end up pulling Naomi away and hanging out with her for half an hour until my vision is blurred and my dick is too fucking hard. She talks about gossip I don't fucking care about, like girls from the cheer team hooking up with my friends. Naomi is the apple in everyone's eye, the token virgin, but I know deep down she's not the good girl she pretends to be.

None of them are.

She peers up at me with her fuck me eyes and I'm tempted, but she is technically underage still. I know she's been waiting for me to kiss her or take her upstairs, but I don't. It's fun having this type of control of girls, and also because Ezra can't rip his eyes off us as we talk, and it's fucking hilarious watching the pure rage seething out of him. I think about his reaction when I finally decide to pull her upstairs and she actually lets me.

I want to see what he'll fucking do about it.

At the very least, hopefully, I'll get my dick sucked. Maison can't be the only one who has fun with a blonde tonight. He's been making out with Olivia on the couch for over an hour. Eventually, they disappear upstairs to one of the spare rooms. She gives him bedroom eyes the whole way up. The little fire whip matched Maison's drinking for most of the night.

I slide my arms around Naomi's waist and grab her ass; she leans up ready for me to kiss her, and I'm just about to when her friend Serena walks up out of nowhere and nudges her. "Naomi, your dad's calling you."

Her phone is buzzing and blinking in her purse and she pulls off me, her eyes shoot open. "Oh shit, I've missed six calls from him." She looks at me and visibly blushes. "I'm sorry, Micah. I have to go. It's way past my curfew."

Fuck. A curfew? Seriously? She's too fucking young and inexperienced for me. I need a girl who can take my shit; I don't want to break them.

And little Naomi Wilson isn't that girl. I can't deal with teasing.

Looks like Maison is the only one getting laid tonight. The rest of the girls here are already hooked up with someone, or I wouldn't touch them, anyway. And I refuse to fucking bottom feed.

Before she leaves, she leans up and whispers in my ear. "Message me later, Micah. I'll be waiting."

Yeah, not fucking likely.

I head outside to go home. I don't want to stay here. I have to get up and train tomorrow because state finals are in a week. Even if these fuckers don't want to get up and work out—I will. I have way too much to lose.

We only live a few blocks away from Ezra's, so I decide to walk to sober up a bit. His house is on a cul-de-sac that backs onto a forest. It's my favorite running trail, and I know it well. And my mood is only worsening by the minute. The tightness I always feel in my chest comes back, and I want to freak the fuck out like the world is going to crash in on me. The same sense of danger I have felt nearly every day since I was eleven.

Watching your twin about to die would fuck up any kid. Getting stuck for forty-eight hours in the wild nearly fucking destroyed me.

When I manage to sleep, I dream about it almost every night. The cold, bitter air still suffocates me. The frostbite still lingers on my fingers and toes. I was weak and helpless and completely unprepared. I promised myself I would never be that weak again. I refuse to even go fishing without a full survival kit.

At least sex helps me get rid of this feeling—it helps me release.

Maison's voice echoes on the street. "Where are you going, Micah?"

I turn to face him. "Home."

"Are you in a mood?"

I shrug. "Nah, man. Enjoy your night."

He's not buying it. He knows when I'm in a funk. He walks toward me and places his arm around me. "You played well tonight, man. The scouts will be back. And you still have all next year. Try to have a good time for once. Celebrate."

I raise my brows. "Why are you out here? Don't you have Olivia waiting? Miss I Don't Have A Boyfriend. What . . . have you banged her already? Or are you just done with her?"

He can't stop the stupid grin from spreading across his face. "Not yet. She wanted to have a shower, so I came down to grab a drink. Then I saw you were leaving."

I gesture toward the house. "Well, don't let me stop you."

He pauses—just long enough to know he's up to something. "You want to have a go at her first?"

Dude.

My blood pumps. This gets my adrenaline spiked.

"Are you being serious?" I ask him.

His face is hard as stone. The same stone-cold look I always have. "Yeah, man. No one will know. I'll stay down here for a bit and be all serious and brooding. Just go upstairs and do your thing. Come down and get me when you're done, and we'll trade spots, then I'll go for round two."

I shake my head but can't shake the throbbing in my dick. "Maison man, I appreciate the thought, but that's over the top, even for me."

He always worries too much about what I might do when I get into my moods. He places his arm on my shoulder. "Come on, Micah. She will calm you down and you know it. She's so drunk she won't even know the difference. And who's to say if it was you hitting on her first, it wouldn't be you she's spreading her legs for right now?"

Fuck. This is so crazy it might actually work. And it will be worth it because Olivia is seriously hot. Maison and I do share everything. Why not this? Plus, it will feel good to fuck the ex-girlfriend of that asshole Fitzgerald. I'll shit talk him about it next time we play them. That will fucking distract him on the ice.

I bite the inside of my cheek. "I don't know, Maison. This feels wrong."

He cocks a brow and gives me his usual smirk. "Last chance, bro. She is seriously hot. She's in bed naked, waiting for one of us. Might as well be you first."

My dick is beyond excited now. All my pent-up adrenaline shoots right to it. I shake my head and walk past him, back toward the house, ignoring his shit-eating grin. "You're such an idiot, Maison."

I can't believe I'm about to do this.

The party has died out. People are either stumbling home, passed out, or still drinking in the kitchen. No one noticed Maison and I switched personas the second we walked back in.

I grab a couple drinks and head upstairs, and Maison heads directly into the kitchen toward a couple of drunk chicks left at the party. I shake my head at him—chances are next time I'll have to at least pretend to remember their names. Whenever we do this, I seem to get a bit more attention and smiles the next few days. I never ask what he says to them, and they never question whether it's him or me.

He seems to be better at being me than I am.

I plant a grin on my face to channel my brother and take a deep breath to control my raging heartbeat. Our whole lives, no one can ever tell us apart unless we want them to. When we turn on the twin thing—it's on.

We mean serious business.

My dick's already throbbing when I hit the top of the stairs of Ezra's dad's mansion. Ezra and his family have relied on our reputation for a long time, and their house isn't as big as ours. His dad's always borrowing money from mine to fund business deals.

The upstairs veers off into two wings, and I hang a left. It's the third guest bedroom in, and always the one Maison crashes in. I make my way through the large hallway, the arched ceilings echoing the voices down below. But I'm alone up here—no one else in sight, which makes me feel better about what I plan on doing.

The bedroom door is open a tiny sliver and I nudge it, trying not to spill the two drinks in my hand. As I step inside the room, she's laying in the bed just as he said she would be, and fuck me, she looks like perfection. A blanket is draped over her stomach, and her tits are hanging out. She has a small smirk on her heart-shaped face. The dim lamp is set on low beside her, and her blonde hair is still damp. She looks at me with her lips over her bottom teeth, and her eyes are glassy.

I can tell by the way Olivia carries herself that she knows what she's doing. And unlike Naomi, at least she's my age. The more experienced, the better. Not a lot of girls in this town can handle my shit, so usually I resort to one-night stands when we travel.

Maison knows me too well. He knows I needed this tonight, and it's much easier for everyone if they catch feelings for him. He handles emotions better than I do, almost like I lost my capability for feeling when I lost all sensation in my hands, toes and ears from being stuck on that lake. I had to turn everything off just to survive it. I never turned it back on. I barely have any emotions, let alone dealing with other people's shit. I'm a terrible boyfriend, but I love getting my dick sucked, so this is a win-win.

Her green eyes blink at me as I walk in. "What took you so long?" she asks.

Yeah, definitely a slur in her voice. Which is a good thing. It's not like she knows Maison all that well. She won't realize we switched. For a tiny second, I pause, and my heart ticks an extra beat. My fucking moral compass is setting off.

Fuck—can I actually do this?

She shifts a bit, causing her tits to bounce, and she smiles at me as my eyes move to her perfectly perky nipples. I'm more of an ass guy, but she's got that going on, too. She has the whole package.

Yeah. I can definitely do this.

I walk over to her and slide in next to her, placing the drinks on the nightstand. "Sorry for keeping you waiting, baby. Micah was leaving, and I wanted to see if he was alright."

Her eyes spark as she picks up the drink and takes a sip. "What's wrong with him, anyway?" she asks.

I tense slightly. What does she mean what's wrong with me? I shrug it off, just a momentary slipup. She wouldn't notice my break in character or how much that fucking stings.

"He gets moody sometimes," I explain, feeling a need to defend myself as I pull off my shirt.

She narrows her eyes but keeps them glued. "But why? He's so mean, but he has so much going for him. Isn't he the star of your team? He shouldn't be like that."

Much better, sweetheart. I *do* have a lot going for me. And I am the fucking star, thanks for noticing. I slide my hand over her stomach, causing her to flinch from my tickling fingers. I remember to soften my touch, even though my urge is to bend her over and fuck her from behind. I can be soft. Sometimes finesse is exactly what girls need, and I know Maison isn't nearly as aggressive as I am.

"He's just misunderstood," I tell her and lean in closer. "He doesn't mean anything by it."

She opens her mouth to say more, and I use the opportunity to kiss her plump lips. I slide my tongue right into her mouth. "Enough about him, baby. I'm all you need right now."

She smiles and leans into the kiss. Fuck, she tastes good—she smells good, too. A fresh-from-the-shower smell, like fucking flowers. Too bad for Maison. He's going to have to fuck her for the first time, smelling like me. I plan on tasting every part of her body before I'm done with her.

I kiss her for a few minutes as she moans and relaxes into the sheets. Her little tongue slips in my mouth, and I grab a handful of her tits and really get a feel for them. I move my lips down her neck and chest and take one of them in my mouth. I'm about to clamp down but stop myself and slide my tongue down her stomach instead toward that glistening pussy waiting for me.

"Maison," she moans into my ear, pressing her body into mine as our kiss deepens, "you feel so good, keep going, don't stop."

Fuck—it should be my name she's calling out. I'm unsure how I feel about the fact it's not, but I don't have too much time to care. She pulls me in harder, and my hands pull down the blanket as I find my way between her legs. She is so horny and ready—Maison, you Casanova.

He's skilled at charming girls, and he barely even gets to know them. When he flashes them a smile, they toss their panties, and he does very little to earn it. Olivia's definitely not wearing anything under that blanket, like she's begging to be fucked by both of us.

I shift and undo the button of my jeans and finally slide them off, appreciating the release of my erection no longer constricted against the fabric. She immediately reaches for my dick as it bulges out of my boxers. Maison already has a condom on the nightstand waiting, so hopefully, he brought two.

I pause for a moment, thinking about the repercussions if she ever were to find out. Would she even care? She's begging me right now so this can't possibly be non-consent, can it? She looked directly at me when she walked over to us. She can play games all she wants, but she knew exactly who I fucking was—twin thing or otherwise.

She watches me carefully, the flush of her cheeks, the flash of her eyes, the recognition in them.

This bitch came to this party for us—she came for me. They always chase me until they realize how complicated I am. But if she saw the game tonight, she knows exactly who I am, since I beat the shit out of her ex-boyfriend. If I really put up a fight and wanted her attention, I bet it would be my name moaning out of her mouth right now instead of my brother's. There is no way she'd be saying no to me, but I need to be sure.

"Are you sure about this, baby?" I ask her. "It's not too fast?" Seems like a sappy thing Maison would say.

She reaches for my boxers and yanks them down, then opens the blanket, letting me in. She gives me those bedroom eyes I saw her give Maison earlier.

"Yes, I'm sure," she whispers. "Get that dick out, Maison, and fuck me."

I slip the condom on and crawl on top of her sexy body. She spreads her legs for me, and I don't overthink it. I slide my dick in her and fuck her hard and quick and say as little as I can while she moans Maison's name the entire time. But fuck it, it gives me the release I needed and craved tonight, and I don't have to deal with any bullshit after either.

It doesn't take me too long to finish. I could have kept going for hours, but that would piss Maison off. When I'm done, we lay panting next to each other and I slam down my drink, which gives me a good excuse to leave as she tries to cuddle.

Sorry, sweetheart. You're going to have to handle round two now.

I put my clothes back on and slip away, heading back downstairs, seeing Maison still in the kitchen chatting with Serena, hopefully pretending to be me. We make eye contact as I walk out the door, feeling a thousand times lighter than I felt walking in.

Thanks, Maison—that was exactly what I needed.

CHAPTER TWO

S he was supposed to be a one-night stand.

This chick lives thirty minutes away in a completely different county. She has her own school, her own people, her own town, but apparently, very few friends because she's been at my house every day since we both fucked her two weeks earlier. Apparently, she and Maison really connected that night, and now she spends nearly every waking moment with him like they are a fucking couple. She just drives up every day in her shitty Honda Civic.

Typical Maison—acting as if what we did wasn't utterly messed up and probably illegal, but Maison is smitten with Olivia and he and I haven't talked about what happened or what he let me do. He hasn't brought it up, and like fuck I will either.

When they are around, I usually hide downstairs in our gym and remember how I'm not even emotionally capable of being with a girl like her, or any girl. Because it's not like Naomi hasn't made it clear that she'd rather date me over Ezra. I could date her in a heartbeat if I wanted to. It's a good excuse to train for the upcoming season and when I'm not training in the gym, I'm at the rink ... practicing. Working out and slicing pucks helps me keep my head clear and my parents off my back for taking myself off medication. People who have this condition have night-mares ... and I just don't fucking sleep.

As soon as I turned eighteen last spring, I got off the meds because it's my body and my choice, even if my parents hate me for it. What happened to me was eight years ago, and somehow, I have to figure out a way to get over it. I wasn't unconscious for it like Maison was—I can't just block it out like he can.

I'm sick of feeling sorry for myself. This is going to be my year, so I have to forget what I did with Olivia and keep myself focused. I barely fucked her the way I wanted, and she could have taken more of me. Forgetting how amazing her pussy felt is easier said than done. When I walk upstairs after my workout, she is roaming around like a lost puppy dog in the kitchen looking for my twin—who's not even here. He went to the lake with Ezra, which means he's there with Naomi and Serena, probably misbehaving as he usually does when he's with them. Two weeks is usually his max with girlfriends, and Olivia's about to hit her expiration date.

I slip past her as she sits on top of the granite kitchen island, combing her fingers through her hair, with her sexy legs crossed in front of her. "He's not here," I mumble as our eyes meet and I immediately look down at my phone, avoiding eye contact before she can give a response. I'm worried if she looks me in the eye, somehow, she will know what I did. That she'll truly recognize me.

I feel her gaze on me as she hops off the island and shifts over to the fridge. "Is it okay if I get a drink while I wait for him?"

I keep my voice neutral even though my dick hardens at the sight of her leaning up with her back toward me, grabbing a glass. "Help yourself," I tell her.

Fuck that—she was waiting for me.

She's wearing a sexy pink bikini with her ass cheeks hanging out of the tiny string, and she's wearing my fucking jersey over top like it's a dress—god fucking damnit. My mom must have put it in Maison's room accidentally. We can afford housekeepers, but my mom insists on doing our laundry even though she's fucking horrible at it.

The jersey says Matei number ten—my number—it's always been my number. Olivia came to a lot of games last year, so she must fucking know that.

She turns to face me and her cheeks blush slightly. "Do you know where he is?" she asks me.

"No."

The words come out harsher than intended, but I'm not Maison's fucking keeper. She presses her lips together and stares at me with her pretty green eyes. The same way she stares at me during our family dinners when she's trying to figure out why I won't look her in the eye.

My eyes glide to her hands as she toys with the hem of her shirt, staring at her pretty nails. Those delicate fingers grazed along my thigh under the table the other night when she sat next to me.

It didn't go unnoticed.

She kept her hand there the whole dinner, while my twin—her fucking boyfriend held onto her thigh on the other side of her. Her little finger slid up and down on the hem of my pants, which caused me the most excruciating boner I've ever had, as I kept thinking what it would feel like having her hands wrapped around my dick.

Her lips twitch into a smile as I can't help myself from staring at her bare legs. She must have known I was looking at her sexy, tight ass while she turned from me.

She arches a brow. "Why didn't you want to go to the lake with everyone, Micah?"

It's the first time she has ever said my name, and a deeply gratifying thrill shoots through me at the sound of it. And I guess I was wrong; she seems to know exactly where Maison is.

I shake my head. "I don't have time for that shit. The pre-season's about to start. I have to stay in shape."

She scoffs and grabs some ice. "You don't have time to have any fun with your friends? Man, you are boring for a hockey star, and the last I checked, it's summer."

I lean my hands back into the counter and take her in fully now. Drinking in all of her as she pours herself some vodka. She looks fucking delicious with my jersey on her like she meant to wear it.

"Not particularly," I say with an edge in my voice. "I don't really like Ezra. My parents make us hang out with him."

Plus, unlike Ezra and Maison who seem perfectly content with how we did at the state finals last week, I am fucking humiliated. Bronze isn't good enough. Bronze won't get me scouted.

She pauses and stares at me and blinks her pretty green eyes a few times before lifting her ass up on the counter. Her pink bikini is all I can stare at now as her trim thighs part slightly with her legs hanging down. My stomach twinges thinking of how tight it was when I slid my dick into her. Fuck, I need to get laid—I haven't done it since her.

She pops a piece of ice in her mouth. "So, tell me, what does New Ocean's top hockey player like to do for fun?"

I give a half shrug. "I don't do fun."

She tilts her head. "Everyone needs to have a little fun. Have a drink with me, Micah." She jerks her chin toward my dad's liquor cabinet. "We should at least get to know each other a bit? I am your twin's girlfriend. And it's like ... I don't know ... you're repulsed by me or something."

The exact opposite, actually, which is the exact fucking problem. I stare at her and frown as I'm tempted to toss one back and not let a pretty girl drink by herself.

Fuck, Maison ... where are you?

She continues swinging those long legs over the counter. "I promise you, Micah," she teases. "I'm really not a good time at all when you get to know me."

Bullshit. I remember how much fun I had with her. I can't stop thinking about it, actually. As if on cue, my phone lights up in my hand.

Maison: If Olivia shows up there, let me know. I ghosted her today.

Me: She's here.

My eyes drift up to Olivia, who's locked in her gaze right at my phone. "Is that Maison?" she asks, still holding her glass, sipping on it. "When will he be back? He's not answering my texts?"

"Yeah, hold on," I tell her, glancing down at my phone.

Maison: Fuck. I'm about twenty minutes away. Cover for me.

Me: I can't cover for you. Sorry, dude. She already knows it's me.

Maison: Tell her I'm in traffic and can't text, but I'll be there when I can.

Me: That's a stupid fucking lie. How did she even get into the house? Did you give her our code?

Maison: Yeah, she sneaks in to see me at night.

Me: What do I get out of it? She's staring at me like I'm supposed to hang out with her. I want to have a shower, and I'm fucking tired. What am I supposed to say to her?

Silence … only those three fucking dots. Then finally …

Maison: Just don't fuck her.

I shake my head, annoyed by how he just can't keep it in his fucking pants, and now it's my problem. He doesn't even like Serena, he's friend zoned her for years. He can't think beyond the moment.

"Where is he?" she asks without missing a beat.

"He says he will be back soon. There's a traffic jam or some shit getting back from the lake. He's with Ezra and his friends from school." I cock my head at her. "Don't worry, sweetheart. He told me to tell you he loves you."

I'm a prick—but at least I'm an honest prick. I don't date for this reason. This shit is too stressful. I can't deal when they get clingy. I'd hate having someone questioning my whereabouts.

She closes her eyes; she knows something is off.

Fuck … I hate seeing girls upset. Damnit, Maison… I take a careful step toward her. "How about that drink?"

Her green eyes immediately light up, and she hops off the counter. My jersey rises again over her thighs as she turns and pulls out a crystal decanter full of vodka.

Fuck, this girl in my jersey.

If Maison hadn't just told me not to fuck his girlfriend, that is exactly what I would want to do right now. She grabs another glass, fills it with ice, pours me two fingers full, and hands it to me. I take it and jump up and sit next to her on the island.

She's close to me now—I don't think I can be this close to her without reacting like I'm some fucking pre-teen with a boner. "What happened with you and Fitzgerald, anyway?" I ask her, taking it down in one full swig, trying to ignore the fact she's staring right at my mouth. "Why bother to drive thirty minutes every day when there are guys in your own town you can fuck?"

The question slips out of me like vomit, but I can't help but ask. Kids from Douglas Cove are poor—rougher around the edges—they stick to themselves; we stick to ourselves.

That's it.

Plus, it wasn't that long ago I saw her wrapping her legs around her boyfriend in the parking lot after the game on his tailgate. That was only like a month ago. She stares up at me through her long lashes and grows quiet.

She finally says in a low voice, "He broke up with me." She bites her lip as if she's ashamed. "Most of my friends took his side in the breakup. I don't have a lot going on back home, to be honest."

Without thinking, I grab a small piece of hair falling in her eyes and tuck it behind her ear. "Why would he break up with a pretty girl like you?"

Fuck ... Maison's rubbing off on me.

She blows out a breath, as if not expecting the compliment. "He got a hockey scholarship to an Ivy League school. I guess I wasn't good enough for him anymore," she says. "He said he doesn't want to be tied down with a girlfriend, especially in his last year of high school, when he knows he will leave next year."

I try to hide the irritation that takes a massive punch right to my pride. Fucking loser-ass Fitzgerald already got a scholarship? Fuck that ...

I shrug. "Who cares about fucking Fitzgerald? Looks like you upgraded with Maison, anyway."

Her eyes gleam and she smiles back ... she liked the compliment. In fact, I think all she wants is my attention. She knew I was home when she came into this kitchen. Instead of hiding in Maison's room, she came out looking all sexy.

She pours me another drink while my heart thuds again. She looks me right in the eyes as she hands it to me. It takes a few seconds to regain my composure enough to grab it from her. We chat for a few minutes. She tells me about her school, her plans to attend community college after—I actually pretend to give a shit.

Finally, the front door bangs open, and Maison barges into the house with girls cackling all around. He appears in the kitchen doorway in shorts with no shirt a few seconds later, typical Maison looking all beefed up. He darts his gaze between the two of us sitting next to each other but immediately smiles at Olivia. I quickly hop off the counter like it's no big deal I am sitting right next to her.

"Hey, baby," he says, walking directly to her and nuzzles his nose into her, "we ran into the girls at the lake and came to grab you." Ezra, Naomi, Serena, and a few others from our team in Ezra's grade follow in behind her.

Maison slides his tongue inside of Olivia's mouth. She leans up and kisses him back, but cuts her eyes to Naomi and Serena, letting them know she's still in the picture. Any tension she had earlier seems to have melted right off.

Maison—the fucking liar. He likely hit on Serena all day, as she watches them make out. Naomi sets her sights right on me as Ezra approaches and snakes his arm around her, pointedly ignoring me. Looks like he and Naomi are back together again, and it's too fucking bad because Naomi's also looking good in those cutoff shorts. Her hair is pulled back tight, and I can imagine yanking on her ponytail as I cum in her mouth, finally exposing this good-girl bullshit persona she puts on.

Damnit ... now that I've had a drink, I'm fucking horny. Maybe I can convince Naomi to sneak away with me. That should piss Ezra right off, and I can finally see what I can make Naomi do for me.

Maison pulls himself off Olivia and shifts his body toward me. He slaps me on the shoulder. "You even got Mr. No Fun to have a drink. Well done, baby."

She looks at me and smiles—that fucking smile. "Micah and I were just getting to know each other a bit."

If Maison sensed anything between us, he doesn't let it show. Instead, he pulls out more booze and heads toward the backyard where the sun is still blazing down outside where my parents have a pool and a whole bar set up.

"Good. Glad he's here instead of the gym for once. Looks like we're going to have a party today since our parents are gone for the weekend."

Olivia jumps up and follows him. Right before she leaves the room, she swivels her head to look at me. For once, I can't read her face, and I can always read chicks' faces. Did I imagine her flirting with me? Was that flirting? I could cut the tension between us with a fucking knife—and it wasn't the bad kind of tension either. This girl is a queen between the sheets. That lazy fuck I gave her a couple weeks ago isn't even half of what this chick can take. I know it. Those were sexy eyes she just gave me.

I tense my jaw, watching them outside as she settles between Maison's legs in a pool lounger. My stomach tenses at the sight of it, however, I can't be jealous right now. Envious—yes. Jealous—no. This girl was never mine. But damn, all I can think of now is how fucking sexy that number ten is on her back.

CHAPTER THREE

Our day party died out pretty early with most people passing out or heading to our theater room to watch a movie. With our parents away, more people came over for a low-key get-together, which turned into a complete booze fest.

I sat back on a pool chair and relaxed for most of it and watched the pretty girls in the pool strutting by me, trying to focus my attention on anybody but the one blonde I shouldn't be looking at. The one who's become a permanent fixture in my brain since our conversation and her blatant flirting with me this afternoon.

Yeah, she was flirting. No question in my mind.

Something's changed. The subtleties of her body language today differ from usual. She sat by the pool, tilting her head and arching her back. Even when she slipped her tongue in Maison's mouth and pressed her tits into him every chance she could, she still made sure I was watching. Her gaze lingered on me longer than it should have.

Don't worry. I'm looking at you, sweetheart.

But she's my brother's girlfriend—this is fucked up. She's not acting right. Even if Maison's eyes wander, too, they are still together. She shouldn't be paying this much attention to me.

Now I can't sleep—not at all. I stare up out my window at the full moon and cloudless night and the row of fir trees that line my front lawn. It's well past midnight. Naomi slipped into my room earlier after Ezra passed out, and I let her cuddle with me for a bit as she asked me endless questions about hockey and what my plans were after high school. I didn't push her to do anything more but kiss. I couldn't bring myself to fuck her yet, so we made out for a few minutes feeling mighty fucking proud of myself knowing her dick boyfriend was in the bedroom down the hall passed out because he can't handle his alcohol.

All the girls I want to have sex with are taken, and all I can really think of is Olivia and how badly I want to slide my dick into her again. My chest tightens, which is a sign I need to get rid of my pent-up energy and sweat out whatever alcohol is still in my system from earlier.

So, I head downstairs for a midnight workout, which isn't unusual for me. What is unusual is when I jog up the stairs when I'm done and she's there. All five-ten of Olivia's gorgeous body sitting on the kitchen island eating a sandwich. A jar of peanut butter and jelly strewn beside her legs as they hang over the side. The light is dim, only the lights on the backsplash from the wall are on behind her; shadows cast over her face. I pause and meet her eyes.

She's wearing my fucking jersey again.

She doesn't look surprised to see me as she takes a bite of her sandwich, licking the bit that falls out the side, drawing my attention right to her lips.

"Is Maison passed out?" I ask her, keeping my tone steady, even though my blood runs straight to my dick.

She nods and swallows her bite of the sandwich.

I fill my water and chug it, wiping the sweat from my brow from my workout. "Isn't it past your bedtime?"

She scoffs and places down her sandwich, swaying a little. "Come on, Micah. Cut the shit."

It was too dim to notice earlier, but she's still drunk. She sways a bit, and her eyes are always glassy when she drinks. I arch my brow and take a couple of steps toward her. "What shit are you referring to? I have a lot of it."

Her eyes zone in on me. "The shit where you pretend you don't find me attractive. I see the way you look at me."

Brazen and beautiful.

I shrug. "So, what if I do? You have a boyfriend, Olivia. I can hear him snoring as we speak."

Our eyes meet, and we engage in a stare-off. I finally shift my gaze down her torso to her jersey—my jersey. Her long, smooth, sexy legs crossed at the ankle, which she happily opens, inviting me in. She knows what she's fucking doing.

I step toward her and lean in. If it's games she wants, games she will get. I press my hands down on either side of her. She flinches, but she lifts her legs and wraps them around me—just like the first night.

I lean my mouth to her ear. "You smell like him. You just fucked him, didn't you?"

She keeps herself steady. "So, what if I did? Would it matter to you?"

I lean back and look at her and arch both my brows. Her legs are spread now and fuck me, she's not even wearing any underwear.

She reeks of sex.

I chew on my bottom lip and ask her, "Maison wasn't enough for you, baby? You need more?"

She snickers, pulling her long blonde hair over her shoulder. I can't even hide my pulsing erection, and she slides her fingers right over it. No more pretending.

"I'm not sure any guy is quite enough for me except you, Micah Matei."

Damn. The way she's been hitting on me, touching me. Following me ...

She came to that party for me. I knew it then, and I know it now. Maison doesn't deserve this, despite screwing around on her.

I clench my jaw. "Is that so?"

She grabs the jar of jelly she left out and grabs a spoonful, rubbing her tongue over it. "You're going to kiss me, Micah."

A bit of it falls on her thigh, and I shake my head. "Go to bed, Olivia. I'm not going to fuck my twin's girlfriend, especially when you're so drunk."

She leans back, opens herself up for me, and slides her fingers in between her legs, rubbing herself. "It didn't stop you before," she says, hitching a breath from the pleasure she's giving herself.

My adrenaline spikes again.

She runs her tongue along her bottom teeth, and she lets out a breathy moan. "That first night, I know it was you who fucked me first. Don't even pretend to deny it."

My usual stone-cold demeanor completely drops at this bomb she's throwing down at me.

How did she fucking know?

"I don't know what you're talking about." My voice literally cracks, watching her play with herself. It's probably the hottest thing I've ever seen.

She licks the rest of her jelly off her spoon, spilling even more of it on herself. This time it falls in between her legs, and my arousal nips at me.

"Come on," she whispers. "It was so obvious. You two are completely different."

I scoff but can't help but run my finger over the jelly on her thigh, bringing it to my fingers to taste it. "You have no fucking idea what you're talking about, sweetheart. You were drunker that night than you are now."

She leans forward and cups my head into her hands, her eyes blaze into me. "If you don't fuck me, I will tell everyone what you did. I will ruin you, Micah."

What the actual fuck.

She runs her hands through my hair, and a smile spreads on her lips. "You definitely won't get into an Ivy League school or the NHL with that kind of charge on your record."

I can't tell what I am more, fucking furious or horny beyond belief. This bitch is blackmailing me into fucking her. My eyes drop to another jelly splotch on her ivory skin, right below the hem of her shirt.

She keeps her gaze on me and runs her hands along my back. "I will keep your secret if you just give me what I want right now."

Annoyance tugs at my gut. "Which is what exactly, Olivia? What do you want from me?"

She flicks her eyes down to the jam mess she's made on herself. "I want you to clean me up to start."

Easy enough.

I lean down and grab her leg, which she lifts to meet my grip. I run my tongue up her thigh, licking up every bit of that strawberry jam off her. My dick gets harder with every second that passes. She runs her fingers through my hair and arches her back. "Now here," she whispers when I'm done and looks down between her legs. My dick twitches, now a painful bulge against my boxers, pushing an ache through my entire body.

She spreads her legs and I lick the bit of jelly right on her folds. I can't help but raise my eyes to watch her as a soft moan escapes her, and she arches her hips, pressing her pussy right into my face. She tastes amazing, so I lick a bit more and her eyes stay closed. Her juices are already pumped up from when Maison fucked her earlier.

I sit up and take a step back, pretending that wasn't the most amazing pussy I've ever tasted. "Done. Can I go to bed now?"

She shakes her head, her eyes flashing with fury. "Screw you, Micah. You don't get to fuck me without permission, then reject me when I actually want it. It doesn't work that way."

I press my arms around her and place them on the island. "That night was a mistake, and you have a boyfriend, as I've said before."

A vicious smile forms on her lips. "So, you don't deny it?"

My face remains neutral, but my heartbeat pulses through my body.

The thrill—it reminds me I'm alive, and I haven't had this feeling in a long, long time. Other than when I'm playing hockey, I never feel this way anymore. It's been forever since a girl turned me on this much.

But still—this is all sorts of fucked up.

"Why are you doing this to us?" I ask her. "Maison is a good guy, even if I'm not. It was my idea to fuck you that night. But why mess with what you could have with him?"

She doesn't need to know it was his idea. I'd rather be the villain.

She slides the jersey up her thigh again, and she shakes her head. "We both know Maison's already cheated on me,

Micah. I'm not stupid. Plus, he told me he needed space tonight."

Was that before or after he fucked her?

She can't have him, so she's coming for me. Or was I always the target? First Fitzgerald breaks up with her, then she mysteriously shows up at one of our parties and zeros in on us.

Olivia Taylor is not an innocent little fucking girl. She's targeting us—this needs to fucking end. Chicks like this can ruin the lives of guys like me, especially given what shithole of a town she's from and that beater car she drives.

Maison's too innocent for a girl like her—he's simple, with simple needs. He should find a wholesome girl like Serena, who believes being naughty means going to parties and flaunting herself while swimming. Olivia is far from the basic girls in New Ocean.

Olivia is another level of crazy.

She kisses me, her soft lips touch mine, and I don't pull away. I've wanted this—couldn't stop thinking about the first time we kissed. This time I don't pretend I'm someone else, and I kiss her back with fury. I slide my tongue into her mouth like she's mine. I sweep my hands right up her body, feeling her smooth skin under the jersey, and I grab hold of her waist. My fingers find her breasts and I squeeze her hard nipples and flick them, and her whole body shudders.

"I want the best, Micah," she moans as she reaches her hand down and grabs my pulsing dick. "And you're the best hockey player I've ever seen, better than Fitzgerald and better than Maison."

I step back and pretend I don't want her, but my fucking dick is betraying me right now. Plus, I wasn't expecting this. I need a feisty girl in the bedroom, and she is playing all the right cards. No one would believe her anyway if she tells anyone what Maison and I did. Not with how fucking willing she is right now. Anyone walking in now would see her legs around me.

I grab her by the hips and press myself into her. Our tongues and teeth mash together as she squeezes tighter.

"You want me?" I ask her, a voice rough. "You want me to fuck you, Olivia?"

I need her to respond yes. No fucking games.

"Yes, Micah," she moans.

The exact name I need to hear.

Maison's snores are carrying through the whole house. I'm not sure how he'd feel about this right now, but he's fucking around on her—and he already let me fuck her once. But he also told me *not* to, like he knew exactly what I wanted to do.

I know I'm breaking our twin code; we don't mess around on each other's girls, but right now I don't fucking care.

She kisses my neck and face as I lift her up. "Not here," I whisper.

I carry her down the hall and into my bedroom. I purposely moved my bedroom last year far away from my brother's. I couldn't stand hearing the chicks' moans when he'd sneak them inside the house.

As we walk, she keeps herself wrapped around me the whole time, licking and kissing me, unfazed by the sweat on my neck from my heavy workout. When we get to my bedroom, I throw her on the bed, and she reaches to pull off the jersey she still has on.

I reach to stop her. "Keep it on," I tell her. "If we're doing this, I want to see my number while I fuck you. Got it?"

She grins and pulls up her jersey, turning on her stomach, pressing out her tight ass. I drop my clothes, put a rubber on, and run my hand up her leg and feel in between her legs. She's already so wet and worn in, so I stroke myself once and slide my dick right inside her as I gather her blonde hair in my hands.

She feels just as good as she did the first time. This time—she will cry out my name in the pillow.

I lean over her and whisper in her ear. "Is this what you want, Olivia? You want the star hockey player fucking you? Screwing your loser ex-boyfriend wasn't good enough. You need both Matei brothers to give it to you, don't you?"

She moans something incomprehensible as I keep giving it to her, not thinking or caring if someone can hear us.

Damn, she's tight and wet and I don't hold back like I did the first time. Since she felt compelled to blackmail me for sex, I will fuck the living shit out of her.

I fall into her back, and she moans every time my dick jackhammers her. After a few minutes, I lay off, giving her a chance to breathe, pulling myself out of her. Most chicks aren't used to my libido, but this girl takes me with ease like her pussy was meant for me.

She wiggles beneath me and turns around to face me. Her heart-shaped face is flushed, and she shuts her eyes as she finds her breath.

"Are you done already?" I ask her, easing the pressure of my muscled body off of her. "This is what you said you wanted."

Her eyes flutter open and meets my gaze through her long lashes. She opens her legs for me as I lay on top of her. My mouth is only a few inches from the silky skin on her neck, so I lap my tongue, careful not to mark her, even though I want to.

"No," she whispers, squeezing her thighs around me, "I'm not done with you, Micah."

She wiggles and slides the jersey up over her shoulders and throws it on the floor next to the bed. And this time I don't stop her. I want the full view of her perky tits and nice round nipples that get me rock hard again. What the hell is Maison thinking, fucking around on this girl? Serena doesn't hold a candle to Olivia.

I lean my forehead in to touch hers. "You want more of me, sweetheart? Because I can do this all fucking night."

"Yeah, Micah," she whispers, wrapping her arms around my neck. "I want you so bad."

Hearing my name makes me come undone. Call me a narcissist, but I need to be the best at everything, fucking girls included. If they are with me, it's me I want them thinking about, during sex, after sex, and always. It needs to be my name out of their fucking mouth.

I slow down as our breaths mingle, and she rolls her hips, taking in every thrust. I pull her legs together and I twist her around to give myself better access and I pick up the pace, feeling her juices drip out of her. I finally feel the tightening in my groin as I play with her tits and cum after about ten minutes of giving it to her like a fucking beast in three different positions. In the final seconds, I yank her around so she's on her back and finish deep inside her while her pretty lips moan my name, and I release all my pent-up tension. Exactly what I needed.

I'm out of breath when we finish and she lies beside me, quiet as a church mouse. I lay my head down and run my hands through my hair.

What the fuck did I just do?

I'm not the only guy in her world. She has a good one just down the hall. Even if he can't get it together and stay loyal to her, he's still pretty amazing.

And what I did wasn't right—deep down I know he would not be okay with this. I observe her as she puts on the jersey, looking for any regret.

"I have to go, Micah. I can't be here when Maison wakes up."

"Yeah, I know." I lean back and rest my arms around my head with my dick still hanging out. She gives me a final glance and a small smile before heading toward the door.

"Hey," I call out to her. She turns and looks at me, furrowing her brows, and I can't help but marvel at her post-sex glow. "Don't tell Maison what just happened."

She scoffs. "Or what, Micah? What will you do?"

I arch my brows and run my hand over my abdomen. "I won't fuck you again, sweetheart."

CHAPTER FOUR

There is a knock at my door just as I finish up with my shower and slip on my white shorts and white-collared shirt.

"Yeah, come in," I mutter, knowing exactly who it is. I'm surprised he even knocked. He usually doesn't—he never used to. He only knocks after we fight, which we haven't done in years.

So, why the fuck is he knocking?

Maison pokes his head in, grinning, and I instantly relax. It's early evening but today's the day of our parents' annual white party. The whole town is coming here for our mid-summer party, and Maison and I are expected to be on our best behavior.

My shoulders relax seeing Maison's grin as if he doesn't have a care in the world. I've been avoiding him the last couple of days, and luckily, he seems oblivious. Or maybe not—since he knocked, so he knows something. But tonight is our night and nothing will stop us. I used to dread this party, but a few years ago, Maison had the idea to dress the same and mess with people all night. My mom's friends love it. They shamelessly flirt with both of us. That's when we decided switching personas was going to be our thing.

He strides in and stands next to me, wearing the same white outfit, and I part my dark hair the same as his and sweep it to the side. He looks good in white—we both do.

"You ready to fuck with people tonight, bro?" he asks, giving my ribs a jab. "Some of the younger girls in this town are looking damn good to me. I might need you to be my wingman, since you don't seem like you are interested in any of them."

I roll my eyes and he adjusts my hair so we match perfectly. I slap his hand away, and we stare at ourselves in the mirror for a few seconds before he says, "Fuck, you are one good-looking dude."

I shake my head, and we both crack up. I swear Maison is the only person in the world who can get me to lighten up. It's me and him against the world as it should be. I'd literally kill anyone who messes with him. I'm the worst person for not telling him what happened with Olivia the night they broke up. And worse, I don't ever plan to.

Olivia hasn't come around for a few days, and I haven't seen her since the incident. Apparently, they really broke up, and Maison assured me he was never committed to her to begin with. He's too immature to admit his mistake with Serena, so breaking up is easier for him. I swear Maison's emotions, while at least he has them, are nothing more than a moth to a flame.

He said he needed to focus more on the upcoming season, which I'm not upset about. He's getting sloppy and slow at training. All of them are—Ezra and the younger kids don't know what's at stake yet and have no idea what losing is like because of me. I doubt they will go to any state championships when I'm not around. The team would be utter shit.

I'm not upset Olivia is not coming around anymore and am relieved I don't have to see her. This is the exact reason I don't get emotionally attached. Girls are way too distracting. At least now she can go back to her ex-boyfriend Fitzgerald and ruin his life instead of fucking with ours.

I match his silly grin and head to the door. "Let's do this, fucker."

By the time we reach the backyard, half the town is already here. All eyes are on us as we enter through the patio doors. My mom has the backyard set up as she always does with her extravagant parties. Our perfectly manicured lawn sits on a high cliff above the ocean, our patio extends all the way to the pool, and my mom has seating areas all throughout, with little tealights that will pop on at dusk. We usually expect around three hundred people, and this year is no exception. It's an event for displaying our wealth with style. This year our food theme is sushi—all white rolls and fresh fish, and the feature cocktails are white bellinis with little umbrellas sticking out of them. She only rambled on about it at every dinner for the past month.

I step on a white balloon, purposely popping it as floats through my feet. The loud bang causes my mom to sharpen her gaze toward me as she's in deep conversation with the mayor's wife.

She gave me a stern warning earlier about my behavior, especially about not fighting or getting into it with Ezra. She knows how much I hate him and how pissed off I was for him stealing my glory goal. She also had to field calls from his mom when I used to beat him up when we were kids. Everyone is still so fucking touchy about me pushing him around when we were younger, and how unhinged I am. The kid is all grown up now. He can take care of himself. Give him a year, he might even be as big as Maison and me.

Ezra and Thomas are talking to a few others on our hockey team, including Naomi and Serena, so Maison nudges me to come with him. I follow him over to the group and try to avoid Naomi's leering stares. When Maison's not with me, he mostly hangs out with Ezra. The two of them have always been close. Ezra keeps his arms locked around Naomi and barely spares me a glance. Naomi gives me a pleading look not to say anything about our make-out session the other night. Guess they are back together, after I never called her like she begged me to.

We are only chatting for a few minutes when I glance up as a tall blonde comes into my view. I flick my gaze toward her and there she is. All five-ten of pure fucking poison. The devil herself dressed like a fucking angel with a short skirt and white tank top that fills out her curves. Her hair waved to perfection.

Damn, she looks good.

I don't recognize anyone she's with—a nerd in a fucking bowtie whose family moved to New Ocean a couple years ago. But why the fuck is Olivia here and speaking to them? Something's not adding up.

Maison pauses mid-sentence when he finally notices her. His body stiffens as she makes eye contact, and she struts over to us without a care in the world, her long legs on full display. He's just as surprised to see her as I am, if his arched eyebrows are any indication. She darts her sexy eyes between the two of us, and it takes every ounce of me not to smirk at her.

Guess it's not so obvious now, is it, sweetheart?

She looks directly at my twin, her eyes soften. "I have family in the area, Maison. Don't be surprised to see me. I was invited."

Shit. Apparently, this girl can see right through us.

"What family?" I chime in and she finally casts her gaze to me after an intense moment passes between the two of them. She's never mentioned family to me, not that we've done much talking.

She blinks at me with zero fucking emotion, unlike whatever just went on between her and my brother. "You wouldn't know him. He's not an athlete, so you wouldn't give him the time of day," she says.

I don't falter my hard exterior even though her iciness cuts deep.

Maison is tense and quiet beside me, and the group quits the conversation and stares at them. Maison finally grabs her hand. "Can we go somewhere and talk, baby?" he asks her.

Baby?

I thought they broke up. What happened to Mr. All The Chicks At This Party Are Looking Damn Hot? A flame ignites in her eyes, and she nods. "Yeah, is there somewhere quiet?"

The two of them wander off, leaving me alone with Ezra and Naomi and the others. I curse under my breath as I pretend not to watch them circle the lawn and disappear behind the house where my parents have a gazebo. Right before they disappear from view, his hand slides to the small of her back, finding the bit of skin above her skirt.

I silence my inner thoughts, and any emotion that seeps its way out of my heart and into my head, reminding myself I have no right to be jealous—

None.

Maison's about to lay it on thick, and with his puppy dog eyes, she doesn't stand a chance when he turns the charm on. I move toward the bar and grab one of my mom's signature white drinks and crush the little umbrella in my fist while slurping it in one gulp. It doesn't take long for my mom's friends to zone in on me, and a tightness forms in my chest.

Fuck.

Maison's my rock at social events; I don't do well at them. And I don't have many people I consider friends.

One of them rubs my arm and asks me all about the upcoming hockey season and how exciting it must be for me to go into my senior year of high school. They eventually get bored with my one-word answers and flutter off, leaving me alone, especially when she sees my fists clenching.

I search the yard and fidget just as Naomi spots me and heads over. Ezra's nowhere in sight, otherwise I doubt she'd be talking to me. "Hi, Micah," she says to me through her fake eyelashes as she walks up, a hesitant smile on her face.

Naomi's looking good tonight, wearing a tight white dress I'm sure her dad wouldn't be too pleased about. Her parents split years ago and can't stand to be in the same room as each other, so I bet her mom's here. I wish I was more into her. Even so, annoyance tightens in my stomach at being second fiddle tonight. Both these bitches were in my bed the other night while their boyfriends slept.

I arch a brow and cross my arms. "Enjoying your night, Naomi?" Uncertainty shines in her face at my underlying tone. She wavers slightly as I step forward, closing the distance between us. "What?" I whisper. "You don't want your boyfriend to see us talking? What if I licked your pretty lips like I did the other night? Do you think he'd like watching?"

She flinches and takes a step back from me.

I'm an asshole—she's young, inexperienced, and experimenting. She's the girl all other girls in her grade want to be—captain of the junior cheer team, and a classic beauty like Olivia.

She probably thinks I'm the guy she should be with. On paper, she should think that. But I'm fucking not. I'm damaged, and she has potential.

"Micah, don't say that." She widens her eyes but keeps herself composed. "Why haven't you called me all summer? I've wanted you to call me."

"Stick with your boyfriend, Naomi," I say, turning away from her just as Ezra sees us talking and pushes his way over to us. I glare at him and get the fuck out of there. Not the drama I need tonight.

Maison and Olivia head toward me, holding hands as I cut through the crowd.

This fucking chick ... seriously. My ego can't take this shit. She gives me a half smile and acts like I didn't fuck the living daylights out of her three nights earlier, and Maison shoots me a *don't you dare ask* look. Fucking guy only thinks with his dick. Not that I'm much better.

I run my hand through my hair, excuse myself, and head back to the bar. Maison and Olivia walk to my parents, holding hands and announce that they are back together.

The night carries on ... I sneak some drinks from the bar and wander around the party, avoiding everyone, until it's an appropriate time to excuse myself. I spot Maison in the crowd and notice him and Olivia sitting alone, cuddled up and exchanging glances and pawing at each other on a patio chair. She's not catching my attention as she did at the pool party.

Fuck this ...

I head inside and restrain myself from punching a wall, but definitely stomp on a stray balloon, aware an outburst wouldn't be appreciated by my parents. I barely make it in the kitchen when Maison's voice carries through the house.

"Micah," he yells.

My body goes rigid, and I turn to face him. The fire inside me is burning strong now. I cock a brow at him. "I thought we were going to fuck shit up tonight. What the fuck is she even doing here?"

He frowns. "Look, man. I like her okay, I'll admit it. We got back together tonight. I'm not planning on messing around on her again. It was a mistake with Serena. I fucked up."

I scoff. "I'm so happy for you."

He pauses and stares at me as if he can see into my soul. Every dark thought, all the primal rage I have hidden within me.

"Fuck. I knew it. You fucked her again, didn't you, Micah?

I freeze.

"Don't lie to me."

I could never lie to Maison, and I can't hide from this either. He brought this on himself the moment he let me have her that first night. I just didn't think I'd want her so badly now. I don't ever think about girls for longer than a fucking day—and since the other night, I can't get this chick out of my head.

He shakes his head. "When did it happen?"

I shrug. "It was the night you broke up with her. She came onto me though, bro. I was minding my business."

"When though? She slept in my bed and was still there when I woke up."

"It was after you fell asleep. I ran into her in the kitchen after my workout."

He wrinkles his brow and pauses. "Are you still having trouble sleeping?"

"Yeah."

Maison wouldn't know how much I really struggle. I hide it well during the day and at night, when my demons come at me full force, he's sleeping like a baby.

He stares at me straight on. "You should go back on the meds."

"Fuck no. That shit fucks with me, man. And you should watch out for that chick. She came to find me thirty seconds after you passed out."

He swallows and bobs his throat as he contemplates what I just said. A moment passes and eventually, he says, "Did it help?"

I flash my eyes at him. "Yeah," I admit. "It's that or hockey. Or lying in my bed staring at the wall feeling like the world caving in on me." It's the most honest I've been with him in months, and he gives me the look I dread the most.

Pity.

A draft of air shoots through the room and noise from the party hits the kitchen and Olivia walks in. She pauses when she sees the two of us, simply parting her lips and adjusting her gorgeous white tight skirt. She is way beyond any other girl here—and she fucking knows it. She walks in knowing she holds both of our attention. High heels and all.

She completely ignores me, which I'm fine with. This just got completely fucking awkward. She wraps her arm around Maison's waist—the safe twin—Maison is the safe one in this situation. I can't blame her.

"Maison, I'm tired," she says. "Can I go lie down in your room?"

He squeezes her waist. "Yeah, baby. I'll be there soon."

She kisses him, darts her gaze at me and slips down the hall. I don't miss the sway in her hips as both of us stare at her backside.

Maison and I face off. We usually don't have uncomfortable silence between us, but I'm not saying a goddamn word.

After a beat, he finally says, "Go, man. Go to her if you want and pretend you're me."

I narrow my eyes. "Are you sure, Maison? Look, if you're catching feels for this girl, we don't have to play this game. I'll back off."

He flexes his jaw. "I just don't want you to catch feels for her, dude. She's my girlfriend, but if it's just sex you need, go for it."

I shake my head, and a heat shoots straight to my gut. "I don't do feelings, bro. You know that."

And I mean every word. This is physical for me.

He gestures toward his room, his face all serious. "Go before I change my mind. I'll be waiting outside."

Fucking Maison—he's selfless to the point of obsession. I'm not fucking worthy of having a brother like him, and I know it's driven by guilt. He still feels it's his fault for what happened to us when we were kids. I told him not to go on that ice. I warned him and he did it, anyway. The ice cracked, and the water pulled him in within seconds. I threw myself in after him without thinking. I saved his life and pulled him out as blood stained the water around us.

Somehow, I kept him alive until we were found. He thinks he's the reason I am the way I am. That it was all his fault for what happened to us out there.

But it's not—it has nothing to do with Maison. Somehow, I think I'd be like this anyway, even if it didn't happen. I don't see the world the way he does. It's not sunshine and rainbows in my mind. It's dark, like walking through shadows in a descension to death.

I step toward his room and keep my face neutral. My stomach tightens, but I'm not going to let it show how excited I am.

I keep my voice even. "I'll try not to wear her out for you, bro."

He snickers. "Oh, don't worry. She will get a piece of me, too. Count on that."

It takes me all of two steps to decide who I want to be when I walk in. No fucking way in hell am I being anyone other than myself.

She's topless when I step in wearing nothing but her silky panties lying over the sheets on Maison's bed. The lights are dimmed, and her tits are perked. She reminds me of how she was positioned the first night I fucked her.

She sits with her back to the headboard and her knees up, accentuating her legs. Her eyes flash for a moment. She has no fucking clue who I am.

Maybe I should just fuck with her? She sure had no problem fucking with me. I take a step forward, and she tilts her head and smiles. "Hi, Micah," she whispers.

She was expecting me.

I jump out of my clothes, saying absolutely fucking nothing. I click off the light and crawl in beside her as she watches me quietly. I slip her panties off, and my fingers find the slickness of her arousal. I kiss her neck and face and she opens herself up to me, enjoying my lips on her skin just as much as I enjoy tasting her.

"Are you ready for me?" I ask her. I always need to be sure.

"Micah," she moans as I slip my tongue inside her mouth. I'm not interested in talking but hearing my name gets me off more than anything. She meets my lips with hers, and once I get her nice and wet, I wrap it up and press myself inside her.

She arches her back and meets my thrusts, wrapping her legs around me. Fuck, she feels good—too good. It's like an addiction.

I'm only mildly irritated thinking if she'd have been this eager for Maison, too, if it were him right now instead of me. The party is still raging outside, and I don't give a shit. There is nowhere else I'd rather be than fucking my brother's girlfriend in his bed while she moans my name.

More or less with his blessing.

I fuck her twice before I leave—again, not saying a word to her and slip down the hall to my room. After a few minutes, I hear her moans again through the vents as Maison finishes her off. I turn to my side, close my eyes, and sleep like a fucking baby.

CHAPTER FIVE

This is how it goes.

On the surface and in the daylight hours, she is with Maison. She's Maison's shiny new toy, and his first real girlfriend. My mom is over the moon excited for them and completely dotes on her. My parents treat her as if she's some national treasure and they are the most spectacular couple in the world.

Maison has finally committed. The golden boy, the easy twin. I ignore the side comments from my mom about how she wishes I'd find someone, too, when the fact of the matter is she's equally mine in the way I need her most.

She spends almost every night here now. My mom says she's fine with it since we are adults now, and she seems to adore Olivia, or at least the version Olivia wants her to see. If you ask me, it's fucking weird. She has her claws so deep on Maison. They are together constantly.

Late at night, and I mean fucking late, she always crawls in with me. Not every night, but most nights. In the darkest hours of the night, she is usually mine. She picks her spots, but I make sure I am always there, waiting for her like a fucking loser. Sometimes I'm asleep already, other times she crawls in, and I wake up to her lips wrapped around my dick.

Either way, it's the time of day I anticipate the most. I get my release, and Maison gets to deal with the emotional shit that comes with having a girlfriend.

We barely speak; we just fuck. She's insatiable and psycho, which I love. In public, we usually act like we can't stand each other, even though she owns me, and she fucking knows it. If Maison knows what we are doing, he doesn't say anything. I'm not even sure he cares. He's getting his dick sucked daily, too.

She's always gone in the morning back with him when I wake up, acting like it didn't even fucking happen. I always get my best sleep when she leaves. It's the only time I can sleep.

Tonight, we are seated around my parents' extravagant dining room table for our mandatory Sunday dinner. The size of our dining table is ridiculous, given there are usually just four of us, but my mom likes to bask in her elegance.

The table seats sixteen people, and Olivia plants herself right across from me and next to Maison.

"Micah." My mom's voice shrills from across the table. I've barely spoken a word as they talk about my mom's upcoming charity event. I've kept my head down all supper, avoiding Olivia's gaze. Plus, I despise the small talk family shit.

"Micah!" My mom's voice escalates.

I whip my head up as annoyance cuts through my chest. "What?"

Her eyes are glued on me from the head of the table. "Did you hear what I just asked you? I asked if you are planning on bringing someone to the gala?"

Everyone is staring at me now, and Olivia's eyes cut right through me.

I shrug. "I dunno. Maybe I'll ask Naomi Wilson."

It's a joke. They know she's dating Ezra, who will also likely be at the gala. I've already decided I'm not going to this stupid party.

My mom narrows her eyes. "Isn't that girl dating Ezra?"

"Don't know. Don't care. It's not like they're married."

My mom dips her chin, giving me the disappointed look I'm used to with her. "Be nice, Micah," she says, as she takes a bite of her roasted carrots. "Naomi is a nice girl, and you really need to find your way with Ezra. Your father has too many business dealings with that family."

So, I'm always reminded. Be nice to Ezra … got it.

My mom continues. "I had lunch with Naomi's mom today. Poor woman … ever since her affair with Charles King, she really hasn't been able to pull herself together."

Naomi's parents went through a very public scandal and divorce when we were younger. Apparently, Charles King gets around town. I'd be surprised if my mom didn't fuck him at one point, too, judging by the gleam in her eye every time she says his name.

"Yeah, Naomi is so nice, isn't she, Micah?" Maison winks at me. I told him about our little make-out session, and he's been encouraging me to hook up with her ever since.

"Enough, Maison," my dad snaps at him. "We don't speak about women like that at this table."

If my dad only knew what Maison and I did to women, or how many of them Maison has been with. He'd be appalled at our behavior.

I keep my eyes glued to my plate, avoiding Olivia. She didn't know about Naomi. I'm uncertain how she'll respond to it happening on the same night.

Her foot slides up my leg, and I finally look at her. Her lips are pursed, and she has a dark twinkle in her eye like she's going to punish me later. Maison is so entranced by his dinner, he doesn't notice our intense interaction as I meet her gaze with fury of my own, my brows arching in response.

This bitch is fucking jealous.

Olivia Taylor doesn't own me. I can date who I want.

Fuck this.

I pull my chair out and excuse myself from the table, ignoring my mom when she asks me what on earth is wrong.

Everything's wrong.

Maison and Olivia head out and I go to the basement to blow off some steam. I might call Naomi over just so Olivia will stay the fuck away from me tonight. This shit is getting weird, even for me.

I shower and lock my bedroom door. Let her chew on that when she comes crawling in later with her panties wet.

I fuck around on my phone for a bit before attempting to sleep when Maison and Olivia get back, and I hear her giggle in the kitchen.

Damn, even her laugh is sexy.

That's something I can't seem to do. I don't make girls smile. I just make them cum repeatedly. I falter when it comes to the cuddly boyfriend shit Maison seems to do with ease. Olivia never laughs with me. In fact, I think we've only said a handful of words to each other. Everyone will be better if I cut this off—I can't see this ending well.

I rise from my bed and unlock the door. Who am I fucking kidding? She will want to see me tonight after that look she gave me.

She comes in later than expected. It's almost 4:00 am by the time my door opens. I stayed awake waiting for her and when I feel her presence at the door, I am beyond irritated. She thinks she's pulling all the strings with me. I shift in the bed as she stands in the doorway wearing my fucking jersey.

My dick stands on end—damnit. Well played, Olivia. Well played.

I sit up and lean back with my hands around my head. I'm wearing only my boxers, but she's not looking at my hard body right now. Her vicious gaze narrows in on my eyes, and she juts her hips out and crosses her arms. Her long blonde hair tied to her side in a loose braid. I imagine pulling on it while she's giving me the blow job I'm about to demand.

"You're not going on a date with Naomi," she says.

I arch a brow. "Aren't I?"

She steps forward, clicking the door shut behind her. "No. You're not. You're mine, Micah."

I pull out my pulsing dick. I might as well get one more blow job out of this. "I don't belong to anyone, sweetheart. Especially not my brother's girlfriend."

She runs her tongue along her bottom lip as crawls up on my bed and kneels at the edge facing me. She lifts her jersey up a few inches, teasing my eyes, and the heat of her gaze nearly has me coming undone.

My cock pulses and twitches, and she smiles. I have to stay strong. I can't fuck her tonight. I can't bring her any sort of pleasure.

"I mean it, Olivia. We are done with these games. No more of this shit."

She twists her mouth. "Yeah," she says as she leans forward and rolls her tongue along my shaft. "We'll see about that, Micah."

She takes me deep in her mouth, and I close my eyes while my body aches from the sensation. I have to grab onto the headboard behind me to keep me in place.

Fuck, this girl can suck.

I involuntarily moan, enjoying the feeling of her taking control like this. After a few minutes, she pulls off me and looks at me. She pulls up her shirt and slides her legs around me, positioning herself to sit right on it.

I have to resist her. This is her power, her way to control. I place my hands around her hips and lift her up, grabbing her braid, pulling her head down to my cock.

"You're not fucking done," I tell her.

Her eyes flicker and her lips twitch with amusement. She thinks this is fun, so I'll show her fun. I run my hand along her face. "Open up, sweetheart."

She opens her lips and takes me back into her mouth. This time she's sitting and I'm the one kneeling over top of her.

I fucking unleash on her.

I face fuck her so hard her eyes water. Then I close my eyes and get lost in it. Every suck, bite, grind. It feels so good, I could almost imagine making her mine for good.

She resists, and every time she tries to pull away, I grab her harder, forcing her mouth on me. Eventually, I explode in her mouth, and it's her whimper that brings me from the black void I'm in.

Fuck.

Opening my eyes, I realize my hands are wrapped around her neck.

I was choking her.

When I let go, she coughs and slaps my dick away. "Fuck you," she breathes, "why did you do that?"

I guess I found her breaking point.

In one fluid motion, I pick her up and spin her around so she's pinned beneath me, and she wiggles beneath my iron grip. "Let go of me, Micah. You're hurting me."

I relent just a little, enough to give her space. I jerk my head to the door. "Get the fuck out and go back to your boyfriend, Olivia. Slide those pretty lips around his dick instead of mine."

She refuses to move, and I find it hard to believe she still wants me after what I just did. "You don't mean that," she says.

"Yes, I fucking do. Don't come back in here again or I will tell everyone what we're doing and what a slut you are. My mom won't be super impressed with you then now, will she?"

The hurt in her eyes kills me, and the bruises I just gave her terrify me.

What I'm capable of when I'm angry.

This isn't all her fault. She might have initiated it to begin with, but I played along, and I kept it going. I wanted it as bad as she did.

She wiggles away, and she saunters to the door.

"You better hurry," I tell her. "Before everyone wakes up and sees you without your panties on." This is the only way I can think of to stop this girl. A girl like Olivia needs a hard stop, and I have to scare her enough, so she never comes back.

She turns to face me and narrows her eyes. She looks fearless now, as she snaps her head at me. "You are going to fucking regret that, Micah."

"What ... hurting you?" Because I already fucking do regret that. In fact, I kind of hate myself right now.

"Breaking up with me," she says, and she slams the door behind her.

CHAPTER SIX

I caved and went to the charity gala. I knew if I didn't my mom wouldn't let me hear the end of it. So, I took Naomi, which accomplishes three things: making my mother happy, getting revenge on Ezra for stealing my goal at hockey, and pissing the mother-loving Christ out of Olivia, which hopefully solidifies the point she needs to leave me the fuck alone. I'm not sure how Olivia hid the bruises I left her a couple nights ago, but she's been suspiciously absent from the house. She is wearing a dress that covers her chest, so I suspect she is doing everything she can to hide them. She wears a shimmery, blue cocktail dress—an expensive one I suspect Maison bought for her.

She's been glaring at me throughout dinner, and it's hard to believe no one else has noticed. I do my best to ignore her, both out of guilt and because she looks so fucking incredible. Her dress hugs every curve. Two people are giving me looks as sharp as razor blades because Ezra ended up bringing Serena as a date, since Naomi broke up with him when I asked her to come with me, and he and his parents are of course sitting at our table.

"Come on, Micah. Let's dance," Naomi leans in and whispers in my ear after dinner ends. We have to endure all the long speeches from the charity CEO, donors, and all the other self-important people who use these events under the guise of charity to improve their public image.

I shrug and place my arm around her, resting my hand on the skin of her blue, backless dress. "Yeah, let's go," I tell her, relieved this dinner from hell is finally over. I rise, aware of all the looks we are getting and loop my arm with hers as only a gentleman should. It's so fake it's fucking ridiculous, but Naomi's beaming.

"We'll dance, too. Come on, baby," Maison grabs Olivia and trails in behind us in the sea of people heading to the dance in their glittery dresses, and I try not to visibly tense.

Once we arrive, the band plays a slow song, and Naomi slips into my arms, and I pull her into me. Her body feels foreign. Dancing is awkward for me, especially since I'm so used to Olivia, who's taller. She's tight though, and I am curious to see what she looks like naked. She didn't let me get too far the other night. I took it easy on her. It's hilarious she thinks she wants to date me, thinking she can handle me.

"What's wrong with Olivia?" Naomi asks me tentatively, pulling her gaze up to meet mine. "It's like she hates you or something. She's weird, Micah. She gives me the creeps, and she's not even from here. What does Maison see in her?"

Does Naomi not have eyes ...

"Because I'm an asshole, Naomi. Or haven't you figured that out yet? Most people don't like me."

She snorts. "Well, I like you, Micah. Why don't you want to date me? I've been giving you hints all summer. Someone like you should have a girlfriend."

I look at Maison and Olivia, and Olivia's usual smile is gone. Every time Maison spins her, she looks at me. Her face entirely unreadable, until my hands slide down Naomi's back and Olivia's lips twitch in response.

It's killing her, seeing me with Naomi. For whatever reason, Olivia is fixated on me.

Both Ezra and Serena seem miserable while dancing together, neither one with who they want.

I look at Naomi, whose big, brown eyes are peering up at me. I pull a loose strand of hair away from her eyes. I lean down and whisper, "You want to know the reason I won't date you, Naomi? I like to fuck, and you're a virgin. That's not appealing to me."

She shifts and her mouth gapes open. "That's the reason you won't date me? I've been saving myself for you, Micah.

I've had a crush on you for years, and you've never even so much as looked at me. I mean, I like Ezra, I do, but I like you more. I won't commit to him until I'm certain I can't be with you."

This catches my attention because I think it's utter bullshit. I always thought Naomi's v-card was her identity. That's how she plays it off.

Pure, innocent, untainted.

She's just like the rest of them—manipulative and crazy. Crazy because she actually thinks she wants to be with me and manipulative because she's lying about something that's clearly important to her.

I grip her hips just enough for her to know she's got my attention and clench my jaw. "Prove it then," I say in a low voice.

She pulls back from me and narrows her eyes. "How am I supposed to prove it? What do you want me to do, fuck you in the bathroom?"

My eyebrows raise and my lips twitch to a small smile.

She hitches a breath. "You're kidding. Here? Right now?"

I lean down and kiss her, taking her by surprise. "Why the fuck not?" I murmur against her mouth. "I have a condom on me if that's what you're worried about. I promise I'll be gentle the first time."

Time to call her bluff ... but seriously, if she does this, I'd fucking date her. Just because her willingness tells me she's probably open to more.

"Fine," she mutters, "let's get it over with then."

Fuck me ... she's being serious.

She takes the lead, pulling me toward the exit of the ballroom. I catch Maison's attention as we walk out, and he merely raises his eyebrows at me as we disappear into the main foyer of the hotel. He's happy about this. He's been pushing me toward Naomi all summer. At least when he isn't letting me screw his girlfriend.

We awkwardly walk through the lavish lobby to reach the men's room. We step inside and I immediately push her up against the wall, pressing my tongue inside her mouth, the throbbing in my groin getting more painful with every second.

I really shouldn't do this ... she's innocent, and I'm just fucking her just to feel a thrill. She pushes me away and narrows her eyes just as I reach for her tits. "If I do this, Micah, you have to promise to date me. I'm not doing this with someone who's not my boyfriend." Her voice is steady, but she's trembling.

She's fucking nervous, and I think I'm unraveling.

What is wrong with me?

I've hit rock fucking bottom, taking a girl's virginity by a urinal, but what am I supposed to do, say no?

I grab her hips and run my hands down her sides to make her feel better. "Yeah, I'll date you, Naomi." I tell her what she wants to hear, and I want to believe the words coming out of my mouth, but they are a lie.

I'll try though, I will seriously fucking try.

She doesn't give me much time to reflect on that thought. She turns around and pulls her hair over her shoulder, revealing her trim back to me. "Unzip it," she whispers.

I shift my gaze toward the door, toward the hundreds of people that could walk in at any moment as I slowly unzip her dress. It falls to the floor, revealing her black bra and panties, and her decent but not magnificent tits and perky ass. I get what Ezra sees in her. She is a cute girl.

I pick her up, and she wraps her legs around me; I find the cleanest place in the bathroom to lean her against, unzip my pants, throw a rubber on, and try to be quick about it knowing I'm making another terrible fucking decision.

CHAPTER SEVEN

Two days have passed since the gala, and Olivia seems to have gotten the hint. She stays at the house with Maison but ignores me and I've locked my door every night just in case. Which also means I have a lot of pent-up energy, since Naomi still has a curfew and she's not allowed over here when she's with her dad, so I haven't fucked her again either.

Olivia was easy. She relieved a lot of that for me; I hadn't realized how much. I never should have agreed to date Naomi. I don't have the emotional capacity to deal with her either. Luckily, the hockey pre-season will hit soon, and training will be in overdrive. I can't see how Maison can keep things up with Olivia. Hopefully, she will disappear and go back to Fitzgerald.

Wishful thinking. Olivia is not the type of girl who will back down. She's cunning, manipulative beyond belief. She trapped Maison and me on night number one. I doubt she will just keep her mouth shut. I'm waiting for the other shoe to drop with her. While I'm stressing out, she's sitting pretty, biding her fucking time. If she accuses me publicly of sexual harassment, it would be over for me. Everyone would believe her. The court of public opinion rarely sides with the accused. And really ... I'm guilty as fuck. The local news would have a field day, and my parents would probably disown me for staining our family name.

Fuck.

I can never do that again. I will never have sex with a girl unless she knows 100 percent it's me she's fucking or without her explicit consent. This was not worth it, and I thought maybe it would be easier to give her what she wants. Still ... I can't be with her just because she's blackmailing me.

It's past ten when I get my gear off, shower, and head out to the empty parking lot of the arena. I stayed at least two hours after the rest of the team left, working on my shot. I think I sliced the puck five hundred times, replaying Olivia's threats in my mind, and regretting screwing Naomi like that when I'm in such a shit headspace. I defiled that girl, and she loved every second.

As I step outside the arena, the warm summer air wraps around me. A thin veil of clouds covers the moon and stars. New Ocean Arena is poorly lit with only one light at the entrance. So, I step carefully toward my car in the empty parking lot just as bright lights shine right in my face. I jump back and squint, dropping my hockey bag.

It's fucking Olivia. I recognize her beat-down Honda Civic. What is she doing here so late? And where is Maison? He practically jumped out of his skates earlier to meet her. I step toward her knowing I shouldn't get in her car, but the little twinge of adrenaline I always feel with her tingles my skin. I can't tell what she's doing because her high beams are blazing right in my eyes.

My car is parked a few feet away, so I walk toward it to drop off my bag. Olivia makes no motions, nothing. She just sits in some weird trance waiting for me. I should get in my car and leave and not get in the car with her. But I know I will.

When I slide in her passenger door, our eyes meet. Something is wrong. She's slumped over, with streaks of mascara running down her face. I swallow a lump in my throat at seeing her like this. Not composed and put together like she usually is.

She's crying.

I fucking hate seeing girls cry. She looks defeated, broken, and out of her damn mind. This chick is anything but sober. Her body sways while she chokes on her breath from crying so hard. Her head turns toward me as I gently touch her bare leg.

Damn, even when she's broken, she still looks amazing in her summer dress.

"Olivia," I say cautiously, "give me your keys; you shouldn't be driving. How much have you had to drink?"

She smirks and pulls the car into gear.

"Olivia, stop."

She does the opposite. She laughs at me and whips the car in reverse.

Fuck, goddamn it.

I lean over and try to pull the keys out, but she's already in motion. She puts the gear in forward and whips onto the street. I lean in and grab the wheel to keep it steady and pull on my seat belt. "Olivia, pull fucking over. Don't do this okay. I'll stay with you; we can keep sneaking around. We don't have to stop being together, but please stop, you're going to get us killed."

I don't mean any of what I just said. I can never have sex with this girl again. We underestimated the extent of how messed up she is. I should have known something was up when Fitzgerald broke up with her. Why else would he break up with the hottest girl I've ever seen?

My voice doesn't seem to land with her. She jerks the car all over the road. This back road goes on for miles, just darkness and trees along the rocky shores. We may end up in the trees or at the cliff's edge if she continues driving like this.

I grab the wheel again. "Let me steer, at least."

"Calm down, Micah," she says as she accelerates the gas. "I'm just driving to Waverly Point. I just want us to talk for a few minutes."

Talk? She wants to talk? About fucking what?

Waverly Point is a two-minute drive from the busy highway and offers an ocean and lighthouse view. It's also popular for teen make-out sessions. Typical small-town shit. As soon as we get there, I'm prying the keys away from her. She slows the car and pulls into the spot, pulls the keys out of the ignition and looks at me.

"What happened, Olivia?" I ask her.

She takes a shallow breath. "I broke up with Maison. I want to be with you, Micah."

My body tightens as her words hit me, and my heart breaks for Maison. She's not lying, I can tell by her body language, the way she's wrapping her arms around herself.

I close my eyes to avoid her penetrating gaze as she waits for my response. This can't happen. How could she think we could ever be together? Maison would never forgive me. I'd lose him over this. He was explicit in what he was offering me, and it was supposed to be physical. She wasn't supposed to fall for me.

I keep my voice soft and delicate. "Olivia, we can't be together."

She crawls over the center console and straddles me, her soft waves falling in her oval face. "Why not, Micah?" she whispers and rolls her hips over me. "You like me. I know you do."

My dick hardens as she grinds herself over it and lets her dress ride up. I wrap my hands and grip her ass on instinct.

Instinct.

Fuck, why does she have to be so hot?

"He's my twin, Olivia. This is betraying him on so many levels."

She presses her lips into mine, and I don't push her away even though I can taste and smell the liquor on her breath. "I want you so bad, Micah," she murmurs in a soft slur. "It should have been you from the start."

That's not true. I've seen her with Maison. She's happy with him. He makes her laugh and smile in a way I never do. If she could have gotten away with having both of us, she would have. She only chose because I forced it.

She deepens her kiss and presses her tits into me, and fuck me, it feels like heaven. Maybe it would have been easier to keep this going. She was being discreet. No one would have known. Ignoring her during the day was easy, and fucking her late at night was bliss.

It was working.

She pulls her lips from mine and slips her finger through the thin layer of fabric she's wearing for underwear and moans my name. She fucking knows how much I love hearing my name.

I pull her lips into mine, our kisses getting even more desperate. My body completely gives way to her. Every part of me is screaming for her now.

She reaches down and pulls open my top button. I wiggle and help her pull my dick out as she slips off her thong, and I can't help but trace my fingers on the yellow bruises on her neck.

The bruises I gave her.

Fuck. This chick will be the death of me. She's a master at seduction, and I play right into it every time. If I do this right now, if I fuck her, I'm drawing a line in the sand. I'll be allowing this girl to put a wedge between me and my brother. I love my brother more than anyone, even my parents.

Maison is like the other side of my soul. A brighter, happier side.

And this chick is the fucking devil.

I pull my lips off her. "Olivia, stop. We can't do this right now. You have to get off me."

I won't hurt her this time ... this time I'll try being soft.

Her eyes are completely glassed over, and she squeezes her legs tighter like she has no intention of getting off me. "Stop? You want me to stop?" she slurs. "You didn't give me that option the first night, Micah."

My body goes rigid. There are those fucking threats again. Her hand wraps around my dick, and it throbs as she strokes it. I shake my head as I watch her work. "You need help, Olivia. Let me drive you home. This isn't normal."

She laughs. "That is priceless coming from you. We are both broken, Micah. That's why we work. That's why our sex is as amazing as it is."

She leans forward and slides her wet pussy right over me and moans as she rolls her body. "You like this, Micah," she whispers in my ear. "I know you do." She presses the button to slide the seat back. "Just let it happen."

I lie back, defeated, as she rides my cock hard. She pants and moans and I rest my hands on her hips, enjoying how amazingly tight she is. I keep my eyes open and watch her. On the outside, she's perfect. Long blonde hair which hangs over her oval face. Thin hips—thick ass and perfect tits. She grabs my hand and moves it to her nipples as she bounces on top of me.

I forget about everything, just her wet pussy and amazing body. When I fuck her, I forget how fucked up I really am. I lose myself inside her.

That's the fucking problem.

She leans forward and whispers in my ear, "I love you, Micah."

Too much—

This is too much. I don't do emotions. I don't do the boyfriend shit, and I've given her no reason to fall in love with me. I've treated her like shit. I even fucking hurt her.

I'm poisonous.

I push her off me and open the passenger door and slip out to take the driver's seat, making sure the keys are tightly gripped in my hand. "We're done, Olivia. Let me drive you home or back to Maison. You don't really love me; you just think you do."

She scoffs and doesn't say anything. If it's at all possible, her eyes look even more glazed, her pupils taking over her entire eyeball like she's on mushrooms or something. She leans and peers out the window, finally understanding what I'm saying. She's so drunk, she can barely lift her head up now. I let her pass out. It's better than what just happened between us.

I slip the keys into the ignition, then run my hands through my hair, debating on where to take her. I should take her back to Maison, but I don't want him to see us together. And I can't take her home because I don't know where the fuck she lives.

"Olivia, you have to wake up and tell me where you live. I can get you close, but you have to tell me what house you live in, okay?"

Silence. Not even a moan escapes from her.

I reach out and grab her shoulder to coax her awake and jolt her, but her head is sunken low and lifeless.

Still nothing.

I hit her harder as I look for a place to safely pull over on the dark country road, and she still doesn't move. "Olivia, wake up. I have to take you home."

I pull over and lean over the console to check on her, and a twinge hits my gut when I see her lifeless eyes staring back at me. Deep emerald eyes—with no fucking life in them. I reach for her neck to feel for a pulse, *anything* to tell me she's still with me. There is nothing, no pulse. Her skin is still warm.

Just like that—she's gone. It's over.

I ignore my racing pulse and weakened muscles; I ignore my inability to breathe. I just stare at her, and the horror of this situation hits me.

She's fucking dead. This pretty girl, who was so full of life, died within minutes of me fucking her. I grab her body and her dead eyes stare back at me, and I cradle her in my arms. Did she really drink that much?

"Fuck, fuck, fuck," the screams come out of me in a way I can't control. I lost control of the situation. I lost control with Olivia. I'm not sure I ever really had any to begin with. I lost it the night I slept with her without telling her who I really was.

And that decision got her killed.

I'm out of breath by the time I pull onto the road, pulling my dark hood over my head in case anyone drives by and sees me. I didn't kill her, I'm positive about that, but will authorities believe me? Especially if they do a test and see my DNA inside her. I'm fucking doomed. No one can find me with her like this. They will fucking crucify me.

I swallow hard and look over at Olivia's slumped body as I drive into the night, away from town as far as I can to think ... figure out what the fuck I'm going to do. My whole body is shaking like I don't have any control over it.

Dumping her body might work. No one saw us together; she would just be reported missing.

NOPE. Can't do that. It will implicate Maison since he was the last person to see her.

GODDAMN IT ... Maison. Did you give her something? It wouldn't be the first time he's done that.

I'm in a dark haze by the time I see the headlights heading straight for us. I go to swerve, then an idea pops into my head. I slam on the brakes and spin the wheel at the last second, losing control of the car. Tires screech, rubber burns, and the car slams into a nearby tree and the car beside us whizzes past, honking like crazy as it misses me by an inch.

My head snaps back and then forward, and the airbag explodes in my face. It was the exact impact I was looking for.

The brutal, near-death kind.

I pause to take a breath and orient myself as the world comes into focus. I realize I'm still alive, and maybe I don't want to be.

I crashed to kill.

The wind is knocked out of me, and my chest feels like it's about to explode, when I register what I heard during the impact. I look over to see Olivia missing from her seat. The impact was hard enough that her dead body slammed right through the glass, shattering it, and now she lies lifeless at the bottom of the tree we smashed into, the headlights shining right on her.

My body trembles as I undo my seat belt and jump out of the hissing car to crawl to her. I shouldn't be moving. My neck and ribs are searing with pain, but I know someone will be here soon, and I must control the sight they see.

The narrative they tell the police.

I grab onto her and huddle over her, cradling her in my arms. I don't even bother to close her eyes. I'm still holding her dead body as someone approaches me from behind. "Holy shit, is she dead?" It's a woman's voice, and I assume it's the lady driving the other vehicle that almost smashed into us.

Yeah, she's fucking dead, you stupid bitch.

I ignore her and drown out everything and just hold this pretty girl in my arms. A girl who didn't deserve an ending like this. I did this to her. She was Maison's and she should have stayed Maison's.

I fucking destroyed her and now this will destroy Maison.

I ignore the sirens and lights as the ambulance and police arrive on scene. I hold her, cradle her, and silently scream. My arms only let go when the EMS pry me away from her.

For some weird fucking reason, they put me on a stretcher, too. They poke at me and tie me up to the bed in the ambulance. I watch in disgust as they put her body in a fucking bag.

No reason to save a corpse.

I close my eyes as they drive me off to the hospital. In an instant, the world crashes in on me as I always suspected it would. I can barely breathe as I think about how badly I just fucked up my life.

And cost Olivia hers.

They keep me at the hospital overnight for observation. My parents visit first. They rush in, asking me all sorts of questions, and my mom can't stop crying or pawing at me.

The police come next and ask me a series of questions. They ask me if I had been drinking and driving, or if I knew Olivia had a blood alcohol content of .20 percent, making her severely fucking drunk. Why I was with her, where we were going, and a bunch of other questions that are none of their business, like the cause of the bruises on her neck. They are going to do a rape kit, and I know exactly what they will find. We didn't use a rubber.

The accident is being investigated as a murder, and I think it actually is.

The only reason I'm not in jail right now is because they tested me and proved I had nothing to drink. I was stone-cold sober when the accident happened, but when they peel back one layer, they have the evidence they need for a clean conviction.

There is no way I am not royally fucked.

I bite my tongue and say nothing, and my dad eventually calls his lawyer.

The police questioned my story multiple times. They will have to investigate any negligence on my part and informed me they will hold me liable for her death if they found any sign of foul play. They will dissect the whole event based on what I told them happened. The doctor came in at that point and shooed the sheriff away.

None of this is looking good for me right now, and I refuse to talk to anyone. I'll stick to my guns on this until the day I fucking die and keep the image of Olivia pure in Maison's mind. He doesn't need to know the ugly side of her. That side of her was just for me.

The nurse gives me a sedative, and I fall into a blissful drug-induced sleep. I'm not sure what time it is when someone kicks my feet. I awake to the hum of the hospital and a beeping sound coming from my bed.

My eyes shoot open and Maison's there, lurking at the end of my bed. His gray hood is up, his face shaded and dark. The pained look in his eyes makes me want to kill myself. Unlike the EMS and police, he asks me a different set of questions. He could give two shits less who was behind the wheel, or the circumstances for why the accident occurred, or even about the accident itself. His question is something much deeper.

"Why did she go see you?" he asks.

I don't respond. What am I supposed to fucking say?

"Why were you with her, Micah? Answer me."

I shake my head as tears sting the back of my eyes. I stay silent, an uncontrollable shudder flows through me. The guilt I feel is heavy. Even if I wanted to say something, no words come through.

Maison's lip quivers, and the emotion pours out of him. "You're a fucking asshole, dude. A selfish ... fucking ... asshole."

As he walks away, I realize my relationship with my twin will never be the same.

About the Author

Rhea Ryan is a spicy writer of romance on the edge of dark and twisty. Her stories are a masterful exploration of the human heart, skillfully navigating the complex and often grey terrain of our inner lives. After writing in the corporate world for over a decade, she realized she had a desire and compulsion to write creatively. She lives in Western Canada with her husband, two young children and a fur baby.

Pretty Little Island is her debut novel.

Follow on Social Media

Instagram: https://www.instagram.com/rhearyanwrites/
Website: www.rhearyan.com
Goodreads: www.goodreads.com/rhearyan
Facebook Group: Rhea's Dark Hearts | Facebook
Newsletter: bit.ly/Rheasnewsletter
Email: rhearyanwrites@gmail.com

ACKNOWLEDGEMENTS

Although Twice Love Burned was born out of the exciting and compelling backstory of Micah and Maison in Pretty Little Island, it was my sister who beta read an early version of Pretty Little Island and said she wanted to know more about Olivia and what really happened between the three of them. That comment led me to writing this novella. So thank you, Sarah, for pushing me to dig deeper.

Special love to my husband and children for your daily patience with me as I follow my dreams. This wouldn't happen without your unwavering support. I know not every day is easy.

To my wonderful beta readers, Abigail Hunter, Melissa Smith (also my editor), and Roxy Leigh. Your talents and time means the world to me and each of you have had more of an impact on this story than you even realize.

OTHER WORKS BY RHEA RYAN

The Bone Love Duet

Pretty Little Island (Book 1)

Torn between two lovers on a pretty but deadly island, London King must survive the ravages of the wilderness and a battle for her heart.My first day at New Ocean Prep was supposed to be a fresh start. A chance to return to my hometown—leaving my ruined life behind me. My goal is simple. Keep my grades up, my head down, and focus on securing my spot in a top journalism program .My past catches up with me as I'm drawn towards the two hottest hockey players in school. A trip to a national hockey tournament in Alaska has me investigating the truth behind what happened to a girl they tormented and killed two summers earlier.This story has more layers than I imagined. The deeper I enter their world, the stronger our bonds become until I can't tell whose side I'm really on.

Sea Queen Reborn

A Dark Fairy Tale Retelling

To discover the truth of my sister's demise, I must infiltrate the legendary Pearl Castle. The home of ancient magic and ruthless Atlantean Kings. Fueled by a thirst for revenge, my path is paved with bloodshed.As I get swept away by the castle's irresistible charms, treachery threatens to expose my true identity and I undergo a transformation that will shape my destiny. Now faced with imminent danger, will love and power be enough to save me from destruction?